Dear Parents,

This is a Stepping Stone Book™ by the Berenstains. We have drawn on decades of experience creating books for children to make these books not only easy to read but also exciting, suspenseful, and meaningful enough to be read over and over again. Our chapter books will include mysteries, life lessons, action and adventure tales, and laugh-out-loud stories. They are written in short sentences and simple language that will take your youngsters happily past beginning readers and into the exciting world of chapter books they can read all by themselves!

Happy reading!

The Berenstains

BOOKS IN THIS SERIES:

The Goofy, Goony Guy
The Haunted Lighthouse
The Runamuck Dog Show
The Wrong Crowd

www.randomhouse.com/kids
www.berenstainbears.com

Library of Congress Cataloging-in-Publication Data
Berenstain, Stan, 1923–
The haunted lighthouse / by Stan & Jan Berenstain.
   p.   cm.
(A stepping stone book)
SUMMARY: When the Berenstain bears vacation in an abandoned lighthouse, mysterious things start to happen.
ISBN 0-375-81269-5 (trade) — ISBN 0-375-91269-X (lib. bdg.)
[1. Bears—Fiction. 2. Lighthouses—Fiction.]
I. Berenstain, Jan, 1923– . II. Title.
PZ7.B4483Beffhf 2001 [Fic]—dc21 00-055310

Printed in the United States of America July 2001
10 9 8 7 6 5 4

THE HAUNTED LIGHTHOUSE

The Berenstains

A STEPPING STONE BOOK™

Random House  New York

"We must be almost there!" said Sister. "I see some seagulls!"

"Yes, we must! I smell the salt air!" said Brother.

"Indeed, we are," said Papa.

It had been a long ride for the Bear family. Soon they would be starting their first seashore vacation.

Their car was packed with seashore things. They were towing a small boat.

Up ahead, there was a bridge. The cubs looked down at the water as they crossed it.

"Is *that* the ocean?" asked Brother.

"No," said Papa. "That's the bay."

"Where's the ocean?" asked Sister.

"It's out there," said Papa. "Just

NOW ENTERING
GULL ISLAND

keep looking. You'll see it soon!"

There was a sign at the end of the bridge. It said NOW ENTERING GULL ISLAND.

Gulls sailed overhead. They filled the air with their laughing cries.

"Why are the gulls laughing?" asked Sister.

"That's just the sound they make," said Papa. "That's why we call them laughing gulls."

"Perhaps they are laughing because Papa did not rent a vacation home ahead of time," said Mama. "So we may not find a place to stay."

"Nonsense," said Papa. "Of course we'll find a place to stay. Stop worrying. We're not here to worry. We're here to have fun. We're here to walk on the beach, to collect shells, to catch fish, and to swim in the ocean."

That sounded fine to the cubs. They had packed all kinds of seashore stuff.

"That's all very well," said Mama. "I just hope we find a place to stay."

"Look! There's the ocean!" cried Sister.

And, sure enough, there it was. Waves crashed and splashed on the shore. Behind each wave came another, and another, and still another. Beyond the waves, the ocean stretched out to meet the sky.

"I can't wait to dive into those waves," said Brother.

"I can't wait to feel the warm sand between my toes," said Sister.

"Papa, may we bury you in the sand?" asked Brother.

"It will be my pleasure," said Papa.

Gull Island was long and narrow. On one side was the ocean. On the other was the bay. There were houses on each side of the road.

"I have been looking," said

Mama. "I haven't seen a single FOR RENT sign yet."

"That's not how it's done, my dear," said Papa. "To rent a house, you go to the real-estate office. They will have lots of fine vacation houses to rent."

"Look!" said Brother. "There's a real-estate office up ahead!"

It was a building with a sign that said MRS. SMITH'S REAL ESTATE.

Papa pulled into the parking lot. The cubs hopped out of the car and ran over to the office.

There were pictures of houses on the big front window. One said BEACHFRONT. Another said SECOND

HOUSE FROM THE BEACH. Another said BAYSIDE—FISH FROM YOUR FRONT PORCH.

"Look, Papa! You were right!" said Sister. "There are lots of houses for rent on Gull Island."

Papa hooked his thumbs in his overall straps. That's what he did when he was feeling braggy.

"I don't want to say, 'I told you so,'" he said. "But I *did* tell you so."

There was a little bell inside the door of the real-estate office. It rang when the Bear family went in. Mrs. Smith was talking on the phone.

"Be with you in a minute," she said. "Please have a seat."

There were chairs around a big

round table. There were two big, thick books on the table. One said BAY HOUSES. One said OCEAN HOUSES.

The cubs began looking through the books.

"Wow, look at these bay houses!" said Brother. "They all have fishing docks!"

"And look at these ocean houses!" said Sister. "They have steps right down to the beach."

"Try to keep calm, cubs," said Papa. "They may not all be for rent."

"Ah, but just about all of them *are* for rent," said Mrs. Smith, who had finished talking on the phone.

"How do you do?" said Papa.

"We're the Bear family."

"Greetings! Welcome to Gull Island!" said Mrs. Smith. "Folks, I have lots of houses to show you. But first, I want to say how glad I am to deal with folks who are smart enough to plan ahead. Just when next summer will you be wanting a house? Next July? Next August? Have you thought about next September? The seashore is lovely in early September."

Papa looked at Mama.

The cubs looked at Papa.

Papa looked at Mrs. Smith.

The word "next" hung heavy in the air.

"Er," said Papa, swallowing hard and looking a little sick. "We don't want a house for *next* summer. We want a house for *this* summer. We want a house right now!"

"Oh, dear," said Mrs. Smith. "I'm sorry to tell you there's not a single house for rent on all of Gull Island!"

Now the whole Bear family swallowed hard and looked sick.

"Not a single house?" said Papa.

"Not a single house," said Mrs. Smith.

Papa felt awful.

Brother felt awful.

Sister looked as if she were about to cry.

It was as if the whole world had clouded over with gloom.

Mama walked over to Papa. She gave his shoulder a little squeeze.

"Now, now, dear," she said. "Don't take it so hard. Let's head back home. There'll be other summers, other vacations."

Brother and Sister led Papa to the door.

Mama followed close behind.

The Bear family looked so sad that Mrs. Smith took pity on them.

"Wait!" she said. "I just might have something for you."

"But you said there wasn't a single house left on all of Gull Island," said Papa.

"That's true," said Mrs. Smith. "The place I'm thinking of is not on Gull Island. It's on Rocky Point Island."

It was as if the sun broke through and chased the gloom away.

"Where's Rocky Point Island?" asked Papa.

"It's not far," said Mrs. Smith. "It's a tiny island just off the tip of Gull Island."

The cubs were overjoyed. They began to jump up and down.

"Yippee, yippee, yay! We found a place to stay!" they cried. "Yippee, yippee, yay! We found a place to stay!"

"Cubs, please calm down," said Mama. "About this house, Mrs. Smith—is it a bay house or an ocean house?"

"Neither," said Mrs. Smith. "It's a lighthouse."

"A *lighthouse*?" the Bear family said with a single voice.

"That's right. It hasn't been in use for years and years," said Mrs. Smith. "Wait. I think I may have a picture of it." She looked through a drawer. "Yes, here it is."

She handed the picture to Mama.

"It's a lighthouse, all right," said Mama.

Indeed it was—a tall lighthouse rising from a rocky island. It was red halfway up and white the rest of the way. Thick beach ivy grew up one side.

"Hmm," said Mama. "I just don't know."

"Please, Mama! Please!" cried the cubs. "May we stay in the light-house? May we? May we? Please!"

"I admit it doesn't have all the comforts of home," said Mrs. Smith.

"What comforts *does* it have?" asked Mama.

"Let me read what's on the back of the picture," said Mrs. Smith.

Mama handed her the picture.

"Hmm," she said. "It has run-ning water. They put it in years ago. There was talk of starting the lighthouse up again. But they never did."

"Why not?" asked Mama.

"Now, let me see," she said. "As I recall, there were a couple of problems. There was no electricity in the lighthouse. You see, they were still using oil when it was shut down many years ago. . . ."

That's when the phone rang.

Mrs. Smith seemed glad for the interruption. At least, it seemed so to Mama.

"A lighthouse using oil?" said Brother.

"That's right," said Papa. "All lighthouses used oil in olden times. But that's okay. This lighthouse may not have electricity. But I'll tell you what it does have. It has excitement! It has adventure! We'll have the vacation of a lifetime!"

"What did you decide about the lighthouse?" asked Mrs. Smith when she got off the phone.

"We'll take it!" said Papa.

"Wonderful!" said Mrs. Smith. "Now, if you'll just sign these papers."

Papa signed the papers.

The cubs were all set for the vacation of a lifetime.

But Mama wasn't so sure. Mrs. Smith saw that Mama was still worried.

"Mrs. Bear," she said, "may I make a suggestion?"

"Please do," said Mama.

"You're going to need some extra things for your stay at the lighthouse. I suggest you stop off at

Barnacle's General Store. It's just up the road."

Mama thanked Mrs. Smith for her advice.

"See?" said Papa as they left the real-estate office. "I *told* you we'd find a place to stay!"

The Bear family piled into their car and headed for the general store.

"Yippee, yippee, yay! We found a place to stay!" cried the cubs.

"Please," said Mama. "You're making so much noise I can't hear myself think."

Mama was working on a list of the things they would need.

Barnacle's General Store sold all kinds of things.

Mr. Barnacle was smiling and friendly.

"Well," he said after helping them find what they needed, "that's everything on your list. Candles, flashlights, batteries, broom, scrub brush, bucket, cleanser."

"Yes, that should do it," said Mama.

"You're sure gonna be ready for a power failure," said Mr. Barnacle. "Er—may I ask where you're going to stay?"

"We're staying at the old lighthouse," said Mama.

Mr. Barnacle's smile was gone in an instant.

"The l-lighthouse?" He paused. "Well," he said, "I guess that explains all the cleanup stuff."

"Yes," said Mama. "They say nobody's lived in the lighthouse for many years."

"That *is* what they say," said Mr. Barnacle. "But if you're gonna stay at the lighthouse, here's a book you should read. Take it as a gift."

"Why, thank you, Mr. Barnacle," said Mama. She looked at the book. It was called *The Secret History of Gull Island*.

Hmm, thought Mama. *Is Mr.*

Barnacle just being nice? Or is there more to it than that?

The Bear family left Barnacle's General Store. Papa and the cubs were filled with excitement as they motored along. Even Mama had begun to relax. What could go wrong on such a beautiful day?

"What's this book?" asked Brother.

"It was a gift from Mr. Barnacle," said Mama.

"Mighty nice of him," said Papa.

"Perhaps," said Mama. "But I have a feeling there was more to it than that."

"Hmm," said Brother. "*The*

23

Secret History of Gull Island."

"What's history, Papa?" asked Sister.

"History," said Papa, "is what happened in the past. As for secrets, folks make up all sorts of stories about these islands. It's good for business. It brings folks to the island. But I wouldn't worry about it."

But Sister couldn't help worrying about it.

Gull Island changed as they rode along. No longer were there houses. Just the road, the choppy bay on one side, and the great ocean on the other.

"I do believe," said Mama, "that the waves are getting bigger."

Mama was right.

"Why are the waves getting bigger?" asked Sister.

"It could be the wind, or there might be a storm out at sea," explained Papa.

The great waves threw up spray as they crashed on the beach. The sun sparkled in the spray. It was very beautiful.

But it was also a little scary.

"What does it say in the book?" asked Sister.

Brother had been reading the book as they rode along.

"I'm not sure you want to know, Sis," said Brother with a grin.

Brother was a pretty good brother. But he did like to tease Sister. One of the things he teased her about was scary, spooky stuff.

"Can't scare *me*," said Sister. "What does it say?"

"It says that pirates sailed these seas," said Brother. "It tells how they came ashore and did terrible things."

Sister felt a little chill. But she didn't let on.

"Brother," said Mama.

"Yes?" said Brother.

"Does the book say anything about the lighthouse?" asked Mama.

"Let me see," said Brother. "Yes, there's a whole chapter."

Brother read to himself. Then he grinned and said, "You *really* don't want to hear about this, Sis."

"Oh, never mind about that,"

ordered Mama. "Just read what it says."

"Okay," said Brother. "But don't say I didn't warn you. The title of the chapter is 'The Haunted Lighthouse.' And that's just for starters."

Brother read aloud: "'The Rocky Point Lighthouse used to be known as the sailor's friend. Like all lighthouses of the day, it used oil. But during one great storm, it ran out of oil. This caused many ships to crash upon the shore. Many sailors lost their lives. The ghosts of those sailors are said to haunt the lighthouse.'"

Sister had had enough. She put

her hands over her ears and hummed so she couldn't hear.

Brother read on. "'Some have wanted to reopen the Rocky Point Lighthouse. But the fear of those ghosts has kept the lighthouse closed to this day.'"

When Brother stopped reading, Sister took her hands away from her ears and stopped humming.

"Hey, here comes the best part, Sis," teased Brother. He leaned forward and started to read some more.

"That will be quite enough, young man," said Papa. "Anyway, it's just as I said. They make up all sorts of silly stories about these islands. A haunted lighthouse, indeed!"

It may have been silly to Papa. But it wasn't silly to Sister.

She knew there were no such things as ghosts. But they worried her anyway.

They had come to a dark woods. The road had become twisty and rough. Great rocks stood on each side of the road. It was pretty spooky.

Suddenly, they were out of the woods and back in the sunshine.

Just ahead lay Rocky Point Island. On it stood the Rocky Point Lighthouse.

It looked just like its picture. It was red halfway up and white the rest of the way. Thick beach ivy grew up one side.

But there was one more thing about it: *It didn't look the least little bit haunted!*

What a relief to the members of the Bear family—especially Sister.

A rickety bridge went from Gull Island to Rocky Point Island. The Bear family's car made its way across.

Papa pulled to a stop beside the lighthouse. The Bear family climbed out of the car and looked around. They looked up at the lighthouse.

It was huge. It stood like a great tower guarding the land against the sea. The glass windows at the top sparkled in the sun.

They looked down at the beautiful white-sand beach. There were steps down to their own boat dock. Great rocks marched down to the sea. Gulls sailed overhead.

"Well, family," said Papa, "what do you think of your vacation home?"

"It's awesome!" said Brother.

"It's like we have our very own island," said Sister.

"Standing around admiring the outside is all very well," said Mama. "But I suggest we have a look at the inside. Get those cleanup things, please. There's going to be a lot of work to do."

Papa and the cubs got the cleanup things.

Mama pushed on the big front door, but it wouldn't open.

"Here, let me do that, my dear," said Papa.

He put his shoulder to the door. It creaked open on rusty hinges.

What the Bear family saw inside was a surprise—especially to Mama.

"Well, I do declare!" said Mama. "It's as clean as a whistle and as neat as a pin. What do you suppose . . . ?"

"Maybe the ghost heard we were coming and swept up," said Brother.

"Never mind the ghost talk,"

said Papa. "No, the answer is simple. This place was closed up so tight that the sand and the dust couldn't get in."

Inside was a big room. It was round. It had a bed, a stove, a sink with an old-fashioned pump, and a table and chairs. There was a little bathroom.

The Bear family stood in the center of the room and looked up.

It was like looking into a long, dark tunnel that went straight up. Stone steps went around and around until they reached the top.

The cubs couldn't wait to start their vacation.

"May we go for a swim?"

"May we dig for clams?"

"May we go fishing?"

"All in good time, my dears," said Mama. "But first we have to unpack. We have to make this old lighthouse comfortable. We have to settle in."

So the Bear family went to work.

They brought in the suitcases.

They made the bed.

"Yippee!" cried the cubs. "There's only one bed! We'll have to sleep in our sleeping bags!"

They got out the dishes.

They got out the food and had lunch.

"I don't know about the rest of you," said Papa after lunch, "but *I'm* going for a swim."

"Count us in!" shouted the cubs.

Mama looked out the window. The waves had gotten even bigger.

"The ocean looks a little too rough for me," said Mama. "But I'll come and watch."

So the Bear family got into their bathing suits and headed for the beach.

"Look!" said Sister. "The gulls are diving for clams."

"Watch what they do next," said Papa.

"They're dropping the clamshells on the rocks," said Brother.

"Why are they doing *that*?" asked Sister.

"To get what's inside, of course," said Papa. "Come, cubs. Help me with the boat."

The boat was heavy. They got it down to the dock and into the water. It was hard work.

"Phew!" said Papa. "What I need now is a dip in the ocean! Come! Last one in is a rotten oyster!"

He ran into the ocean. A big wave knocked him down.

The cubs ran into the ocean. Another big wave knocked them down.

Mama watched as they splashed in the ocean.

But Mama wasn't the only one watching. Someone, or some*thing*, was watching . . . from a secret hiding place between the rocks!

Brother and Sister felt good after their swim. Sister was helping Mama with supper.

Brother went back to reading *The Secret History of Gull Island*.

There was more about the ghosts. It told how they howled at night. Brother could almost hear them.

He looked at the steps that curved around the lighthouse. He wondered what was at the top.

"May we climb the steps, Mama?" he asked.

"Perhaps," said Mama. "But not until after supper."

But something happened during supper that changed Mama's mind.

A big clamshell came bouncing down the steps. It broke into bits on the stone floor.

"The g-g-ghost!" said Sister.

"I don't think so," said Papa. "I'm sure there's a better explanation. Come. We will climb the steps and find out."

Papa led the way up. Mama and the cubs were close behind.

There was a door at the top. Papa pushed it open. Creaking, it opened on a room. It was round like the one downstairs. It had large windows. One of them was open.

There was nobody in the room.

"If this is a lighthouse, *where* is the light?" asked Brother.

"You're looking at it," said Papa.

All Brother could see was a row of big mirrors.

"How did it work?" asked Sister.

"There was an extra big oil lamp in front of the mirrors," said Papa. "The reflection made a powerful light. Sailors could see it through the darkest storm."

"That's all very well," said Mama. "But I think I can explain the clamshell."

Papa and the cubs had forgotten about the clamshell.

"It's very simple," said Mama. "Somebody was up here cooking clams."

She pointed to some empty clamshells on the floor.

"Maybe it *was* the ghost," said Brother.

"A ghost that eats clams?" said Mama. "I don't think so."

"But how did they get up here?" asked Papa. "They didn't climb the stairs."

"That's also very simple," said Mama. "They came in through this open window."

"That's impossible," Papa said. "This window is a hundred feet high."

"It may be impossible," said Mama, "but that's what happened. Perhaps, Papa, you have a *better* explanation."

"As a matter of fact, I do," said Papa. "If you'll look out the window, please."

Mama looked out the window.

"What do you see?" asked Papa.

"I see gulls dropping clams on the rocks to get what's inside."

"Exactly," said Papa. "That's where the clamshells came from. Gulls were trying to smash them against the lighthouse. But some came in the window. One of them came down the steps. The gulls ate the clams and left. Now, if you'll excuse me, I'm going down to finish my supper."

Mystery solved.

But Mama wasn't so sure.

6

It was the middle of the night. Brother was twisting and turning in his sleeping bag. He was having a dream.

He dreamed he was in a haunted lighthouse.

He dreamed there were ghosts howling at the top of the lighthouse. The howling got so loud it woke him up.

The trouble was, he *was* in a haunted lighthouse. Ghosts *were* howling at the top of the lighthouse.

Brother was frightened. He climbed out of his sleeping bag and jumped in bed with Mama and Papa.

"I was here first," said Sister.

There's room for everybody," said Papa.

"What's that awful howling?" said Brother.

"I'll explain it in the morning," said Papa. "Now please go to sleep."

Mama and Papa were already making breakfast when the cubs woke up the next morning.

"Well, how are my little ghost jumpers this morning?" said Papa.

The cubs rubbed the sleep out of their eyes.

"What about that howling?" asked Sister.

"I heard it," said Papa, smiling.

"If it wasn't ghosts, what was it?" asked Brother.

Papa went to the trash can. He took out an empty bottle.

"It was the wind," he said. "Watch." He put the top of the bottle to his lips and blew.

It made a *Who-o-o* sound.

"It didn't sound like that," said Brother.

"It sounded like ghosts," said Sister.

"This is only a small bottle," said Papa. "There's a big chimney on top of this lighthouse. It wasn't ghosts that were howling. It was the wind blowing across the chimney."

The cubs hoped Papa was right.

"Time to wash up for breakfast, cubs," said Mama.

"And be quick about it," said Papa. "We're going fishing. Gonna catch our lunch."

The cubs washed up in the little bathroom.

Mama went to the window.

"I like the idea of fresh fish," Mama said. "But I don't like the looks of that sky. There's a storm coming. It looks like a big one."

"Don't worry, Mama," said Papa. "We'll just zip out there and catch us some fish before the storm even knows we're there."

Down to the dock they went.

Papa carried the fishing pole.

Brother carried the tackle box.

Sister carried the hamper to put fish in.

The sky was dark and gloomy. But Papa and the cubs looked cheery in their orange life jackets.

They climbed into the boat. Papa stood at the back.

He pulled the starter cord.

The motor started with a roar.

The boat left a white wake as it headed out into the ocean. The ocean was choppy.

"Look!" said Brother. "There's a boat coming out of the bay!"

"It's a fishing boat," said Papa. "She's the *Mary Lou*."

The sailors waved.

Papa and the cubs waved back.

"Papa," said Sister, "I see some lightning out there."

Papa started counting. When he got to seven, they heard thunder.

"That means the storm is seven miles away," said Papa. "Let's drop anchor. We'll start fishing now."

Brother dropped the anchor. It took a while to hit bottom.

Papa held his fishing pole. He unlocked the reel. The lead weight took his line to the bottom.

"Do you think you'll catch anything?" asked Sister.

"I'd better," said Papa. "I promised Mama fresh fish for lunch."

"What are you trying to catch?" asked Brother.

"I'm trying for flounder," said Papa. "They're bottom feeders. I hope we catch one soon. That storm is looking bad."

"Any nibbles?" asked Sister after a minute.

"Not so far," said Papa, "but wait. I think I've got one! It must be a biggie!"

Papa began to reel in. He had to wind hard. There was something heavy on the line.

The cubs began to get excited.

"Stay seated!" shouted Papa. "We don't want to lose anybody overboard!"

Papa kept winding.

"This must be the *biggest* flounder in the whole ocean!" he shouted as he kept on winding.

"I see something!" cried Brother. "It's bigger than you, Papa! *It's bigger than the whole boat!*"

That's when the great creature rose out of the water.

It was a giant ray.

It tried to shake the hook loose. When it couldn't, it turned and headed out to sea. It was a powerful swimmer.

"We've lost our anchor!" cried Brother.

"Hang on!" shouted Papa. He held on to the fishing pole for dear life. It was his best pole. He didn't want to lose it.

"It's pulling us out to sea!" cried Brother.

"What should we do?" cried Sister.

"We'd better do *something*," shouted Papa. "Or this fellow will have *us* for lunch!"

Up ahead, the sky was black with storm clouds. Lightning flashed across the sky.

"In my tackle box!" shouted Papa. "Get the scissors! Cut the line!"

But before Brother could find the scissors, the boat stopped dead in the water.

The giant ray had broken the line.

Papa slumped.

His arms were shaking.

His whole body was shaking.

Their wild ride was over.

And were they ever glad!

They rested for a few minutes.

"I hate to go back without fish," said Papa. "But that storm is coming in fast."

Papa shut off the motor. The boat nosed up to the dock. Papa jumped out.

"Give me a hand, cubs!" he said. "The storm will bring high tides. We must pull the boat up on the rocks."

The cubs climbed out. They helped Papa.

Mama was waiting in front of the lighthouse.

"Hello!" she called. "Did you catch anything?"

"I'm afraid not. But you should have seen the one we got away from!" Papa said with a grin.

They pulled the boat up on the rocks. It was hard work.

"Phew!" said Papa.

"Oh, dear," said Mama. "You left your fishing things in the boat. I'll get them. You need a rest."

She went to get the gear.

"What's this? Your little joke?" said Mama when she came back.

She took a fish out of the hamper. She held it up by the tail.

It was a big, beautiful flounder.

"Huh?" said Papa. "Er, yes, it's my little joke. Isn't that right, cubs?"

"If you say so, Papa," said Brother.

"That's right," said Sister.

Where had the fish come from? This time, Papa had no ready explanation. But wherever it came from, it went down great.

It was delicious.

After dinner, Mama looked out the window. The sky was still black. Lightning was still flashing. Thunder was still rolling. But the wind had died down.

"This must be the calm before the storm," said Mama. "Papa, we're almost out of wood for the stove. It's bound to rain soon. Would you gather some wood before it does?"

"Sure thing," said Papa.

"May we go along?" asked Brother.

"Yes, but don't wander off," said Mama. "The storm is coming."

Papa looked for firewood on the beach.

The cubs did wander off. They climbed on the rocks.

"Let's pretend we're mountain climbers!" said Brother.

"We'll explore!" said Sister.

They climbed the biggest rock. It *was* like a mountain. When they reached the top, they saw a truly amazing sight.

Before them lay a graveyard of wrecked ships.

"Wow!" said Brother. "It's just

like it said in the book. These are the ships that crashed when the lighthouse failed."

There were dozens of them. They were all topsy-turvy. Some were almost whole. Others were in bits. Years in the sun and salt spray had bleached them ghost white.

Sister pulled at Brother's shirt.

"This is scary," she said. "Let's go back."

"Okay," said Brother. "But there's wood here. Much better than the wood Papa's getting. Let's take some back for the stove."

They slid down onto the deck of one of the wrecked ships.

There was a cracking sound.

"YI-I-I-PE!" they screamed as the deck gave way.

They dropped like sandbags and landed with a thump.

They were in a ship's cabin.

They tried to get up. They couldn't. The floor was slanty like the crooked room in a fun house.

At one end of the cabin was a desk. Someone was seated at it.

8

"Nice of you to drop in," he said. He wore a captain's hat. He was old. He had a white beard.

"Y-y-you must be the g-g-ghost," said Sister.

"And you must be the cubs that moved into my lighthouse."

"*Your* lighthouse?" said Brother.

The old fellow came over to the cubs. He had no trouble walking on the slanty floor. He helped the cubs up.

"Captain Salt here," he said.
"Keeper of the lighthouse until
those fools ashore shut 'er down.
Been watchin' over 'er ever since."

"Are you the one who put the fish in our hamper?" asked Brother.

"Yep," said Captain Salt, "tossed it in while you were rasslin' with your boat."

"Are you the one cooking clams in the tower?" asked Sister.

"Right again," said Captain Salt.

"Excuse me, Captain," said Sister. "But why did you throw that clam down the steps at us?"

"Did no such thing," said Captain Salt. "It was an accident. I was openin' 'er and she got away."

"How did you get up to the tower?" asked Brother. "You didn't climb the steps."

"Climbed up the outside," said Captain Salt.

"Climbed up the sea ivy?" said Brother. "It would never hold you."

"There's iron handholds hidden in the ivy, son. You go up 'em just like a ladder. Came down the same way. I may be old, but I'm spry!"

"It was *you* who cleaned the place!" said Brother.

"I keep 'er shipshape at all times," said the old captain. "Those fools ashore might decide to open 'er up at any time. I want to be ready. But let's get out from under this hole you made. Rain's comin' in."

That's when the storm hit hard.

The rain poured into the cabin.

There was a huge thunderclap.
There was the sound of a foghorn.
But it wasn't just going *BO-O-O-P!*
It was making three shorts, three
longs, and three shorts.

"That's the *Mary Lou!*" shouted
Captain Salt. "It's the SOS call! She's
in trouble."

9

"We saw her heading out to sea yesterday," said Brother.

"Those fools!" cried the captain. "They knew about the storm! Here, take these oilskins. Follow me!"

"We don't need raincoats, sir," said Brother.

"They're not for you!" cried the captain. "They're for the wood!"

The cubs didn't understand. But they followed the captain up the cabin steps.

"Into the deck cabin!" shouted the captain. "There's dry wood!"

The cubs still didn't understand.

"Do what I do!" he ordered.

He spread a raincoat out on the floor.

The cubs did the same.

Then he piled wood on it. Next he buttoned it and tied the bottom.

The cubs did the same. Now they had three bundles of dry wood.

Next the captain took hold of the sleeves.

The cubs did the same. Lightning flashed. Thunder crashed.

Then it was as dark as night.

"Let's go!" cried the captain.

He charged out of the cabin with his bundle on his back. "There's not a second to lose! The *Mary Lou* is in desperate danger."

He dragged his bundle up onto the rocks.

"To the lighthouse!" he cried.

Now the cubs understood. They were right behind him with their bundles on their backs.

Papa saw them coming.

He pointed to Captain Salt. "Who's this?" he shouted.

"We'll explain later!" cried the cubs.

"To the tower!" cried the captain.

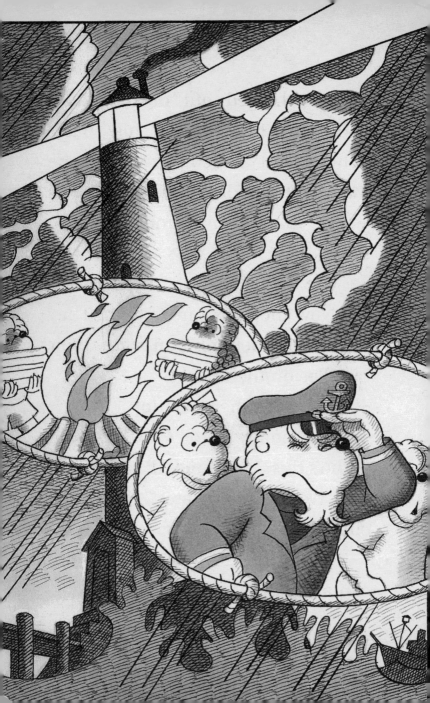

"Do what he says," said Mama. "I think I know who he is."

The captain was bounding up the steps. Papa grabbed the cubs' bundles and followed. Mama and the cubs were close behind. When they reached the top, Captain Salt was already hard at work.

"Look!" cried Brother. "He's building a bonfire in front of the mirrors."

"Yes!" cried Sister. "The *Mary Lou* will see it. She will steer away from the rocks!"

The bonfire was ablaze. The mirrors reflected its light out to sea.

"More wood!" cried Captain Salt.

Papa and the cubs went down for the stove wood.

Up they climbed with big arm-loads of wood.

"Onto the fire!" cried Captain Salt.

They piled the wood onto the fire. The blazing fire crackled and roared. Outside, the storm roared even louder.

Captain Salt looked out to sea. "I see 'er light!" he cried. "But she's still heading for the rocks. More wood! Bigger fire!"

"There *isn't* any more wood!" cried Papa.

"The table and chairs!" cried Brother.

Back down the steps went Papa and the cubs. Back up again they came with the table and chairs.

"Onto the fire!" cried the captain.

The bonfire roared and crackled.

The captain cried: "I think they've seen it! Yes! They're goin' to miss the rocks!"

"Listen!" said Sister. "The foghorn is different now! Three shorts and a long!"

"That, my dear," said the captain, "is V for 'victory.' The *Mary Lou* is saved!"

They were all exhausted. They sat on the floor and watched the great bonfire burn down.

"Phew!" said Papa.

"That goes double for me," said Brother.

"That goes triple for me," said Sister.

"May we introduce ourselves?" said Mama. "We're Mama and Papa Bear. You've already met our cubs."

"Captain Salt here, ma'am," said the captain. "Keeper of this lighthouse—until these fools ashore shut 'er down. But now we've saved the *Mary Lou*. Perhaps those fools will start it up again."

Next morning, the sun rose in a cloudless sky.

The waves lapped gently.

The breeze was mild.

The air was soft and sweet.

It was as if the storm had *never* happened!

It was a new day for the Bear family. And a new vacation.

They swam.

They fished.

They clammed.

They crabbed.

They collected shells.

They buried Papa in the sand. It took a lot of sand. But they managed it.

They visited with Captain Salt.

He told them stories.

He brought them a table and some chairs from one of the wrecks.

Finally, it was time to go home.

They put the boat on the trailer.

They packed the car.

They cleaned the lighthouse until it was just as they had found it.

Captain Salt came to say good-bye. "The lighthouse and I enjoyed your visit very much," he said. "And you were a great help in saving the *Mary Lou.*"

He shook hands with Papa, Mama, and Brother. He leaned down and kissed Sister.

His whiskers tickled.

She giggled.

"We want to thank you for everything, Captain," said Mama.

The Bear family piled into the car and buckled up. With waves and good-byes, they pulled away.

They went back across the rickety bridge to Gull Island.

They went back down Gull Island Road.

They went back over the long bridge to the mainland.

"We'll be going back to school soon," said Brother. "And we always have to write about how we spent our summer vacation."

"Well," said Papa, "you've got *quite* a story to tell."

Brother thought about that.

"There's just one problem," he said.

"What's that?" asked Papa.

"Nobody will believe it," said Brother.

Papa thought about that.

"The lad's got a point," he said with a shrug.

The Bear family's vacation had been exciting.

But their tree house was home. It didn't take long to settle in.

About a week before school began, the mailbear delivered a package.

"Guess who this is from?" said Mama.

Mama showed them the return address.

It said:

CAPTAIN SALT

ROCKY POINT LIGHTHOUSE

ROCKY POINT ISLAND

Inside was a letter. Mama read it aloud. "'Dear Bear family: Big things have happened. They would not have happened without your help. With sincere thanks, Captain Salt. P.S. Those fools ashore have seen the light. They have reopened the lighthouse. The newspapers printed the story.'"

Mama shook out the envelope. There was a newspaper clipping inside. The picture showed Captain Salt standing in front of a sign. It said ROCKY POINT LIGHTHOUSE—THE LIGHTHOUSE THAT CAME BACK TO LIFE.

"Look!" said Brother. "There's the lighthouse in the background."

Mama read from the story: "'Captain Salt is once again keeper of the Rocky Point Lighthouse. With the help of a visiting family—'"

"Hey! That's us!" said Sister.

"'With the help of a visiting family,'" continued Mama, "'Captain Salt saved the *Mary Lou*. He did it by building a bonfire in the lighthouse tower. "It was black as night," said Captain Starkie of the *Mary Lou*. "Without that light, we'd have crashed for sure." The Rocky Point Lighthouse now has a powerful electric light. It can be seen for miles.'"

"Hey," said Brother. "Now I can write about how I spent my summer vacation. Folks will have to believe it. This clipping is proof."

The Bear family had the clipping framed. It hangs on their living room wall. They look at it often. It reminds them of their stay at the haunted lighthouse.

Sister still gets a little chill when she thinks about it.

But she also smiles.